Mysteries In Merrysville

SUE'S MYSTERIOUS VISIT!

BY
AUNTIE COCO

Illustrated by Nicole W.
New York, NY 10001

This book is dedicated to:
My Dear Mother Maria, My Husband,Turtle, Bobby and Dudie.

ISBN: 979-8-89283-216-8

Coco's Cozy Book Nook, Inc.
Printed in the USA
209 W 29th St. New York, NY 10001

Table Of Contents

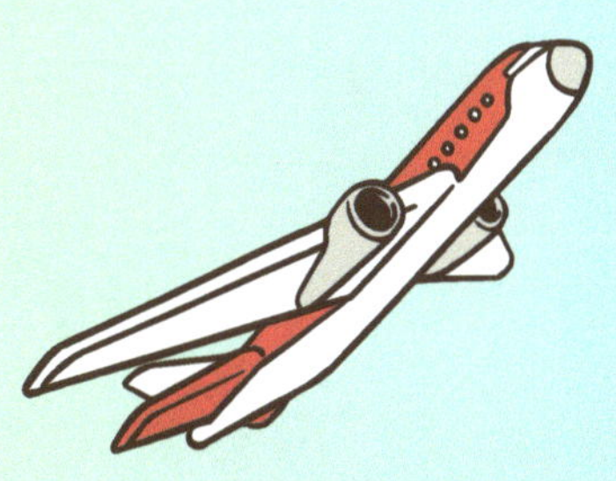

CHAPTER 1

The Clumsy Thief

Sue was from Merrysville, but she lived in New York City. She visited her mother, warmly called Mother Pearl by all, every summer. Visiting mother is going to be so much fun, Sue thought to herself as she packed her favorite things.

Sue took a plane to Merrysville. There were people moving all over in the airport. Some seemed to be in a hurry, while some were not. Some people were waiting to pick up their loved ones, and some were waiting for their flights to be announced.

This airport looks so busy; I wonder if everyone remembered to pack everything that they will need for their trip. I wonder where all of these people are going. Sue thought.

When Sue finally got to her seat, she was lucky to get a good window seat. Sue bought some yummy chocolate-covered marshmallows, her favorite, for the trip. Then she got all cozy in her seat and began to read one of her favorite detective books.

As the plane flew higher and higher, from her window, she could see huge mountains, fluffy clouds, and the beautiful blue ocean. Sue grew tired after reading her book, so she took a long nap. When she awakened, Sue was excited to see that she had arrived in Merrysville.

Mother Pearl was to pick up Sue at the airport. Sue looked at her wristwatch while waiting for Mother Pearl at the airport. She searched through the crowd wondering why Mother Pearl was taking so long. Then she spotted her. "Mother!" Sue cried happily as she waved at her mother.

Sue and Mother Pearl hugged; they were so happy to see each other.
"I'm glad you made it, Sue." Mother Pearl said.
"I am so happy to see you, Mother." Sue said.
"I am too." Mother Pearl replied, smiling.

They took a trip to Merrysville farmers market; the place was filled with people.
Everyone seemed to be in a hurry; there were people moving up and down.
There were various shops and food stalls selling various items.

Mother Pearl and Sue wanted to buy some flour, eggs, butter and a bag of
sugar.
They were shopping for ingredients for the annual baking contest,
which will be held at the state fair later that week.

"Help!" Someone suddenly screamed. A woman in a pink dress was screaming and crying. She was pointing at a man who was running away, holding a pink purse. The purse belonged to the woman, and the man was the thief who had taken it from her.

Sue felt sorry for the woman; she brought out a whistle from her bag. She blew the whistle.

"Stop that man! He is a thief!" Sue cried. "Stop him!"

A policeman who was sleeping in front of a shop heard Sue's voice and woke up.
He started running after the thief, but he wasn't fast enough.

The thief had almost made it out of the market,
but he suddenly tripped and fell into a pool of water.

SPLISH!   SPLASH!   SPLAT!   OUCH!

The policeman caught the thief and returned the purse to the woman.

The woman was so happy, and she thanked Sue for her help.
"What are you shopping for?" The woman asked.
"We are shopping for ingredients for the annual baking contest at the state fair." Mother Pearl replied. "You have helped me; I will also return the favor." The woman said, "I have a shop, and I sell the ingredients that you need."

The woman gave them a bag of sugar, some flour, and all they needed to make blueberry pie. She refused to accept money for all she had given them. Sue and Mother Pearl thanked her.

CHAPTER 2

Midnight Noises

Then they drove home, talking about the strange event which had taken place at the market. "You've always been a blessing to everyone around you." Mother Pearl said,
"Thanks to you the thief was caught, and the woman got her purse back." Sue and Mother Pearl finally arrived home.

Sue and Mother Pearl sipped tea and talked excitedly about winning the annual baking contest. Mother Pearl had always won the first prize, and she was really looking forward to winning the first prize again.

Both Mother Pearl and Sue talked for a while until they both decided to go to bed. They said good night and went into their rooms.

In the middle of the night, Sue was awakened by a loud crashing sound.
She was wondering where the sound came from when a knock sounded on
her door. Mother Pearl entered her room looking worried.
She had also been woken up by the sound.
"I was awakened by a loud sound." Mother Pearl said. "Me too."

"I think it came from the living room." Mother Pearl said.
They both went into the living room, but there was nothing there.
"Let's check the kitchen."

Mother Pearl picked up a broomstick, and they both walked towards the kitchen. When they got into the kitchen, they realized the sound was coming from another part of the house.
"Oh dear, what could be making so much noise?" Mother Pearl asked aloud. "I wonder what it is." Sue said. "Let's check the garden."

They went into the garden, but they found nothing. Then they searched the study room and the laundry room, but there was nothing there either. They were tired, sleepy and worried.
"Oh look!" Sue suddenly cried.

There were muddy paw prints all over the living room floor.

"What is that?" Mother Pearl asked, "Oh, they are paw prints! There's an animal in the house."
"How did it get in?" Sue asked with fear.
"It must have climbed in through that window." Mother Pearl said, pointing to an open window.
"Oh no! We left the window open. What should we do?"
"Let's look for it. Where could it be?" Mother Pearl asked, tiredly.

They continued with the search, following the paw prints which led them
to the attic.
They got flashlights to look for the animal.
There were so many old items in the attic, and the animal seemed to have
been trapped between them. Sue and Mother Pearl started moving some
of the old things
out of their way as they kept searching. "Meow!"
"There it is!" Mother Pearl cried, moving some old furniture aside.
A cat had been trapped between the furniture.

"Poor Cat!" Sue said.
The cat ran out of the attic; they ran after it.
It climbed out through the open window and ran into the garden.

"Poor thing. It must have been so scared." Mother Pearl said.
"Yes." Sue agreed. Mother Pearl yawned.
"Let's go back to bed." Sue said.

CHAPTER 3

The Baking Contest-Flossie's Fib

The smell of Mother Pearl's famous blueberry pie filled the whole house. Her grandmother had shared the recipe with her, and she had always cherished it. Flossie had often asked for the blueberry pie recipe, but Mother Pearl never told her. This secret recipe had always won Mother Pearl the first prize at the state fair baking contest, and she was looking forward to winning the first prize again. The doorbell rang, and Sue went to see who was at the door. It was Flossie, Mother Pearl's friend.

Flossie had also made a blueberry pie for the contest, but hers had turned out badly.

"Oh my," Flossie said, "Mother Pearl your pie smells so good."

"Thank you." Mother Pearl said.

"We are running late, let's get dressed." Sue said, walking out of the kitchen.

"I will be right back, Flossie." Mother Pearl said, walking out of the kitchen too.

Flossie looked at Mother Pearl's blueberry pie with envy. She had always wanted to win the baking contest, but Mother Pearl had always taken the prize. She wondered how it would feel to be the winner, to receive the prize and all the praise.

She would switch the pies and win the first prize, she thought.

She quickly ran outside where her car was parked. She took Mother Pearl's blueberry pie and replaced it with her soggy blueberry pie. She took Mother Pearl's blueberry pie into her car and returned to the kitchen with the pie that she made. A few minutes later, both Sue and Mother Pearl walked to the kitchen to get Mother Pearl's blueberry pie to take to the baking contest. They carried the soggy blueberry pie with them, and they all left for the fair. When they got to the fair, it was bubbling with activities.

The judges were already seated, and the contestants were lined up.
Mother Pearl and Flossie joined the contestants.
"Hello everyone, I welcome you to this year's annual baking contest." The
moderator said. "I want you all to pick a number. When your number is
called, you will come up here and present whatever it is you have made.
Each of the judges will have a taste of it, and at the end of it all they will
decide who the winner is."

The moderator declared the contest open.
He called each of the contestants, and they all made their presentations.

Then it was time to announce the winner. Everyone was worried, they were all restless. There was silence now as all eyes were on Mother Pearl because her famous' Blueberry pie had always won her the competition.

Sue held Mother Pearl's hand nervously. She whispered to her that all would be alright. "Based on the decision of the judges, the best pie is a blueberry pie.
And the winner is..." The moderator paused. "Mother Pearl,
I just know that you're going to win." Sue whispered again.

"You think so?" Mother Pearl asked, worriedly.
She had realized that the pie looked a bit soggy on the way to the fair.
"Yes, you have the best recipe ever!" Said Sue.

"I'm afraid the pie looks a little soggy." Mother Pearl Said,
"I don't know what went wrong."
Sue wondered to herself what could have gone wrong.
She knew that Mother Pearl had always baked perfect blueberry pies and that her pies had always won first prize unless if someone had...

"The winner is Flossie!" The moderator said. "Flossie come forward and received your prize. Congratulations." Flossie screamed with excitement. She ran forward and accepted the prize as a round of applause sounded. Mother Pearl stared at her in surprise, she had known Flossie for a long time, and she knew she made terrible pies. She was sure something had gone wrong; she thought Flossie had played a dirty trick on her.

Before Mother Pearl could stop her, Sue walked up to her.
"Stop." Sue said, "I am certain the pie Flossie presented was not hers but
Mother Pearl's." There was a loud gasp of surprise from everyone.
"That's not true!" Flossie cried. Her face was red with shame.

"I can prove that you cheated." Sue said.
"Can you tell us how you made the blueberry pie and the secret ingredient that you used?"
Flossie looked down at her feet. She had no idea how Mother Pearl had made the blueberry pie.

"How did you make the pie, Flossie?" The moderator asked.
"Yes, tell us!" Everyone yelled.
"I...well...I used eggs and..." Flossie said and then started crying. "I'm sorry. I switched the pies; I have always wanted to win the first prize. I presented Mother Pearl's blueberry pie as my own."
Flossie ran out in shame.

The first prize was given to Mother Pearl again, and everyone cheered for her.

Sue's Surprise Welcome Home Party

Mother Pearl and Sue drove back home. Sue noticed Mother Pearl's street was strangely filled with parked cars. "Why are there so many cars parked on your street?" Sue asked as they got to the street. "I guess my neighbors have a party going on." Mother Pearl replied. "Oh, I suppose so."

They got out of the car and walked towards the house. However, before she could bring out her keys from her bag, Mother Pearl's door was surprisingly found open. They both stopped at the door, afraid to enter. "Something is not right." Mother Pearl said with her voice a little shaky.

She took Sue by the right hand, making her stumble a bit. Immediately, they headed for the back door leading to the kitchen to see if it wasn't locked. "Maybe we should call the police," said Sue. "No, not yet, let's find out what's wrong before calling the police." Said Mother Pearl.

They were both scared and afraid because they were not sure what strange thing they might find in the house; whether or not someone had broken in. Sue got up enough courage and held the door's handle, turned it down and noticed it was locked. Mother Pearl gave her the keys, and she slowly opened the door. Sue was the first to walk in, and Mother Pearl followed behind.

They were very quiet while taking their steps so as not to make a noise. The house was very quiet, but they noticed something; all the lights were turned on. "I didn't leave the lights on." Mother Pearl said, but Sue made a sign to her to be silent. She agreed.

Then they followed a path leading to the living room, and as Sue's right foot stepped into the living room, something strange occurred! Several loud voices were raised together all at once, "Surprise!!!" That was when Sue noticed what had been happening all along.

The living room was filled with family and friends. They were all smiling happily.
"Welcome home, Sue." They all shouted.
Sue was surprised, and she was very happy that her family and friends had gone through so much trouble to throw a "Welcome Home Party" for her.

The house had been decorated colorfully with balloons. Sue got hugs and gifts from everyone: they all said that they had missed her so much and they were really glad that she was back in Merrysville for a weekend visit.

Sue laughed happily, as she was glad to see her niece Alisia, her aunt Betty and her uncle Bernie, her brothers and everyone she held so dear. Mother Pearl told everyone what had happened at the farmer's market and the state fair, and they celebrated Sue for her wisdom and courage.

There were lots of goodies to eat; a cake had also been baked specially for her. Sue had so much fun, and she took a lot of pictures with her family and friends. The party ended in the evening, and everyone hugged Sue goodbye. Mother Pearl and Sue cleared the table after everyone had left. Sue realized that she really had such a good time.

Sue was going back to New York City the following day, so she went into her room to pack her bags. The next morning, Mother Pearl drove her to the airport.

"I really had so much fun, Mother." Sue said. "I'm glad you did." Mother Pearl replied as she hugged and kissed her goodbye. Mother Pearl waved at her until she disappeared out of her sight.

Sue took her seat on the plane, smiling as she thought to herself just how much she really enjoyed her weekend in Merrysville.

The End.